Davey's Hanukkah Golem

To Grandpa's girls:
Tara, Gabrielle, Erin, Amanda, and Sarah

Library of Congress Cataloging-in-Publication Data
Gantz, David.
    Davey's Hanukkah golem/by David Gantz.—1st ed.
        p.   cm.
    Summary: Fascinated by his grandfather's telling of the legend of
the golem, Davey makes himself a golem out of cave clay as his own
secret Hanukkah miracle.
    ISBN 0–8276–0380–0
    [1. Golem—Fiction.   2. Jews—Fiction.   3. Hanukkah—Fiction.]
I. Title.
PZ7.G1535Dav   1991
[E]—dc20   91–2328
                                                  CIP
                                                   AC

Davey's Hanukkah Golem

The Jewish Publication Society
Philadelphia — New York
5752-1991

by David Gantz

Davey's father was a baker. He worked at
night to bake bread for the following day.

Every morning Grandpa and Davey waited for him to come home with bags full of delicious bread and rolls.

Then Grandpa and Davey would sit at the kitchen table. While they ate their rolls and butter, Grandpa would tell delightful tales of dybbuks and goblins. Davey liked the legend "The Golem" best. Although he knew the story by heart, he always asked Grandpa to tell it again and again.

And Grandpa would begin. "A long time ago, the Jews in the ghetto of the old city of Prague were threatened by an angry mob. When the Rabbi Yehuda Lev Ben Bezalel learned about this, he modeled the likeness of a man out of sacred clay." Grandpa would tell Davey how the rabbi spoke the same holy words with which the heavens and earth had been created and breathed life into the clay.

"And that's how the golem was made," Davey would interrupt, "and he grew into a giant and protected the Jews from their enemies."

The morning before the first night of Hanukkah, Davey's father carried home a large, strange-looking package along with the usual bag of bread and rolls.

"This is for tonight," he said. Then he put it next to his bed and went to sleep until late afternoon. That night, after the family lighted the first Hanukkah candle, Davey cut the string and unwrapped the package. It was a bright, shiny red scooter! Davey was so surprised and excited that all he managed to say was, "Wow!"

The next morning Davey carried his scooter down the three flights of stairs to the street. The air was crisp and clear as Davey rode down Stebbins Avenue past the synagogue and past Postofsky's Junkyard.

"That's some scooter, Davey," said Mr. Kurtz as Davey glided past his fruit store.

Davey was having a grand time riding his scooter, when he heard a voice call out, "Hey, kid!" He turned around and saw two older boys on homemade skate scooters coming toward him. But Davey took off before he could hear one of them ask, "Do you want to have a race?"

The two boys thought he had accepted their challenge, and they raced after him. But Davey was afraid they were chasing him because they wanted his scooter.

Davey raced recklessly across Boston Road, dodging neighing horses, honking autos, and clanging trolleys. Then, turning to see if the two boys were gaining on him, he bumped into the "I Cash Clothes" man and scattered his wares all over the street.

Determined to win the race, the two boys on skate scooters raced through the scattered clothes in hot pursuit. Davey scooted into Crotona Park. He was heading for a place that he and his friends called Canyon Rock. *I'll be safe in our secret cave beneath Canyon Rock,* Davey thought as he raced on.

Davey got to Canyon Rock well ahead of the boys on the skate scooters. He quickly crawled into the cave's narrow opening. His scooter couldn't fit so he left it outside, hidden behind a tree. Not long afterward, the boys reached the cave and stood there bewildered.

"Look," said one. "He must have crawled into that cave."

"I guess the race is over," said the other. "Let's go."

As Davey crawled deeper into the cave he smelled the musty odor of the clay that Grandpa had so often described in his legend of the golem. Davey followed the dank smell until he sniffed out its source.

Davey started playing with the clay. He shaped a figure out of it, a figure of the golem. As he became more and more absorbed in modeling the clay, he forgot about the two boys on skate scooters. Not until he was finished making the figure did he realize how long he had been in the cave. Then he remembered the boys outside.

Davey crawled out of the cave.
He held up his clay golem and
shouted, "This will protect me!"
His shouting scattered a flock of
crows. By the time their flapping
wings had stopped making noise,
Davey saw that the two boys
were gone.

"You saved me," Davey told
his golem. Then he saw his
scooter, right where he had left it.
"And you saved my scooter, too!"

Davey raced through the darkening woods of Crotona Park. He remembered that Mama had told him to be home before dark in time to light the second night's Hanukkah candles.

The candles in Grandpa's menorah were already lit. Mama had just struck a match to light the center shamash candle of her menorah, when Davey came rushing into the apartment. Davey's own menorah was waiting for him. He was glad that no one asked him where he had been. He patted his pocket. The golem was his own secret Hanukkah miracle.

Davey loved his new scooter. He rode it every day.

On the eighth and last day of Hanukkah Davey joined Grandpa on his morning walk. "I have a Hanukkah present for you, Grandpa," Davey said, as he pulled a small package out of his pocket.

Grandpa unwrapped his gift and smiled. Under the layers of paper was a little clay figure.

Temple Israel
Minneapolis, Minnesota

BEST WISHES FOR
A SPEEDY RECOVERY TO
DR. ALBERT GREENBERG
FROM
ROSE SCHLEIFF